Unofficial

DIARY OF
A ROBLOX NOOB

PIGGY

RKID BOOKS

CONTENTS

Prologue

A Bear Trap in More Ways Than One.

When faced with your imminent end, a lot of thoughts run through your mind. Good thoughts, bad thoughts, crazy thoughts... Your mind just goes haywire. I guess that's just the way it is. I mean, when you're at the edge and you just know you're about to die, what else can you do but think?

I'm getting ahead of myself, though. How about we get to know each other first? Check out this QR code, and then we'll get back to the story.

So there I was with the gleaming steel bear trap clamped firmly onto my leg. Its large metal claws had popped up out of nowhere, obscured by the shadows. And now I was in agony. Imagine the feeling of falling down a flight of stairs that's covered in Legos, then landing on a trampoline with even more Legos, then being launched into a pit of Legos—all while it's raining Legos. Oh, and they're made of steel.

Anyway, the trap bit into these blocky legs of mine, and I was going nowhere.

"Help! I can't move! Help! Somebody!" I screamed, but no one answered. I tried to tug my leg free, twisting and sweating with the effort, but with every move I made, the trap just seemed to clamp down harder. The room was so dark that I had walked right into one of Piggy's infamous traps, and by the time my brain kicked in, it was too late.

Everyone in Roblox has heard stories of how players dragged into Piggy's home have stumbled upon—or right into—those nasty traps. Some of them never make it out of the first trap alive—and that's all part of the fun for that crazy porcine killer.

That was one list I really didn't want to land on.

There was no way I was moving from that spot. Just when I thought things couldn't get any worse, I suddenly heard a low growl from a short distance in front of me. The growl didn't sound welcoming at all.

The room I had entered was dimly lit, its darkness concealing the bear trap. Now, I was starting to realize that there was more than just the bear trap to worry about. I looked straight ahead and saw two red eyes staring back at me from the darkness. I didn't think things could get worse after getting stuck in a bear trap and desperately needing to use the toilet.

"Uh oh."

Slowly, the animal emerged from the darkness. I could see it a lot clearer now, and I realized what it was. It was a large bear. The bear was huge in stature, but it was actually pretty thin. I could see its ribs sticking out from its fur. Its mouth was frothing, dripping with saliva, and it was staring right at me. This animal had not eaten for a long time, and I was its next meal.

The bear was looking right at me now, and I could hear its stomach growl with anticipation. My leg was still held painfully in place by the bear trap. Nope, this was not good. In fact, it was one of the scariest situations I had ever found myself in.

Scarier than the time I forgot to buy my mom a gift on Mother's Day.

"Nice bear. Nice bear. You wouldn't want to eat me. There are a lot of high-level Roblox players out there. They're fatter, have a lot more meat, and would taste a lot better too. And..."

The bear cut me off with a ferocious snarl.

It flashed its claws towards me, and I could see just how sharp they were. Images of being chewed up and digested by that hairy monster ran quickly through my head, and I screamed out desperately for help.

"No, no! Help! Decks! Dan! Tina! Anyone! Help me!"

Suddenly, everything seemed to be happening in slow motion. The bear was still rushing right at me, but it seemed to be slowing to a crawl.

One thought kept running through my mind: *How* had I gotten into this mess?!

Entry #1

The Mysterious House

I've played more than my fair share of games across tons of Roblox servers, and I've seen all kinds of stuff, from the weird to the wild to everything in between. But I'd *never* played anything like Piggy, which was, without a doubt, the creepiest and nuttiest game in Roblox.

I hadn't even meant to play. The game just sucked me and a bunch of other players into it, and that's where our story and my scariest ever diary begins (OK, yeah, it's my first diary. But still!).

So how did I end up playing Piggy? I didn't really want to play Piggy at all. I had heard scary stories about this game. While other servers were cities or even worlds that were larger than life, I'd heard that Piggy was nothing more than a house.

It was a *big* house, and the size only made it scarier. Players regularly got lost and never returned once they were inside the place. I'd also heard about players getting sucked into the house for no reason. Apparently, the house was drawing players into itself like some kind of vacuum cleaner or black hole. No one really knew what type of force was at fault, but it was there, and it was doing its dirty work.

Like all terrible experiences you hear about after the fact, I didn't really pay much attention to any of it while it was happening. Then again, isn't that always the story of my little Roblox life? Trust me—you'll see.

I was in the middle of playing Mad City when it happened. Yeah, Mad City was another pretty crazy server at Roblox. I had heard about how there were a lot of gangs in Mad City that were always at odds with the cops.

For my first day in Mad City, I enlisted at the Mad City police department to get some action going. Yeah, I know it was a pretty crazy idea trying to be a cop, especially in Mad City of all places! My partner, Kenny, liked to chat a lot, and he always had two things with him: his pistol and a doughnut. He often had both in each hand, which meant that he was an awful driver.

It was my first routine patrol, and Kenny was driving the squad car while I sat beside him. I had no idea how the car could support both of us: Kenny was a heavyweight of sorts, and it showed with his round belly. His belly was so big that you could serve Christmas dinner on it.

"So, what's up, rookie?" Kenny asked.

"It's Noob, not rookie."

"Same thing to me. Want some doughnuts?"

Kenny offered me a bite of his half-eaten doughnut. I could see the grease, chocolate, and custard filling dripping down the sides. Kenny was getting a lot of grease on his hand as he held that half-eaten thing. He was the expert on doughnuts. I think maybe in a past life he was one. It was anything but appetizing. Of course, I declined.

"Uh, no thanks! I'll pass on that."

Kenny shrugged. He probably didn't even want to share the doughnut.

"Hey, food is food. You're going to need a lot of food to get through Mad City, believe me."

I thought that was an odd thing to say. I guess Kenny ate to pass the time when there wasn't a crime. The man was practically a human trash bin.

That was when we heard a shot ring out.

"There you go! Just what I was talking about. There's never a dull moment in this town, kid!"

"That sounded pretty close by."

"I think it came from the hardware store at the corner of the block."

Kenny had an unusual radar-type sense for these things. We turned the corner and saw two perps holding up the hardware store, just like Kenny had said.

"Whoa! How did you know it was here?"

"You get used to these things when you've worked here as long as I have. And a doughnut helps. A lot."

I would have to take Kenny's advice a little more seriously. We stepped out of the car and grabbed our guns; it was time to get to work. Kenny quickly shoved the rest of the doughnut into his mouth like a starved pelican.

"Mad City Police! Drop your weapons! Come out of the store with your hands up!"

I shouted the command at the perps with as much authority and intimidation as I could muster. I sounded confident, but I was shaking in my boots. I was so nervous that I farted. I hoped Kenny didn't notice.

"We ain't coming outside for no coppers!"

Well, so much for negotiations. The perps were crouching behind the front desk of the hardware store. I wasn't sure if the owner had been hurt or not.

Kenny and I stood outside the store, using the wall for cover. We waited, ready for anything.

"This looks bad. Stay sharp," Kenny ordered. The perps started firing first. The bullets whizzed past us, but we couldn't stay there forever. We had to make a move.

I stepped out from behind the wall and fired a few shots back. Their bullets came a lot closer to me than I would have preferred.

"Are you trying to get yourself killed?" Kenny shouted. "Those perps are playing for keeps! Stay covered. I'll dash back to the car and radio for some backup. I think we'll need it."

I heard Kenny, but I couldn't just stand there and do nothing. Well, actually I probably could have, but I was feeling reckless. As a veteran cop in one of the most notorious cities in Roblox, Kenny gave great advice. Advice that I definitely should have listened to, but I didn't. Maybe I should have tried that doughnut after all...

I stepped out from my cover and tried to fire again. Just imagine! A brand-new cop at Mad City stopping a robbery his first day. I would be a hero! I would be famous! I would get a million friends! Or a million Robux. Either one would suit me fine.

Yeah, keep dreaming, Noob. This time, I paid for my brashness. I felt the shot hit me, knocking me backwards.

I lost consciousness and everything went black. The last thing I heard was Kenny's voice.

"What did you do, Noob? I told you to stay covered!"

Before I lost consciousness, I just knew I was done for, and I had no one to blame but myself...

I did wake up, though—with a major headache. My head felt like someone had played several games of soccer with it, and I could barely get up. It was like taking a bath in Lego bricks.

Somehow, I managed to open my eyes and take a look around me.

"Ouch! My head! What happened? Wait, I remember! I just got shot! I'm supposed to be outside the hardware store. Where am I?"

I definitely wasn't outside the hardware store anymore. Instead, I was inside what appeared to be an old, rotting house. The paint on the walls was peeling off, and the floorboards looked so unstable and creaky that I was reluctant to stand on them. There were cobwebs everywhere, and I thought I would choke with all the dust in the air. On the opposite wall, a pair of shattered windows were boarded up, and the bulb above us flickered on and off, barely giving out any light. What kind of place was this?

There were several other players in the room too. Like me, they were all just waking up. One of them was even pretty famous. I had seen him play in several servers, and he often liked to post vids about his game experiences.

"Danny SN? Is that you? What are you doing here?"

"Hey, aren't you Noob?"

He actually recognized me! Despite meeting in such a scary situation, I found that very cool. I was really surprised that a famous Roblox-er like Danny SN knew me. For a moment, all my confusion and tension vanished.

"Whoa! You recognize me? I mean, you're Danny SN!"

"And you're Noob! I mean, I played a in few servers you were in. I've actually bumped into you before, and I've got to say I liked what I saw back then."

This was better than Christmas and my birthday combined.

"Thanks, Danny! I'm surprised you even remember me."

"I try to make a point of remembering every player I play with. After all, we're all really just trying to have fun, right?"

One of the other players in the house spoke up. "Sorry to disappoint you guys, but I don't think we're going to have fun here. I'm pretty sure this is Piggy's house!"

She sounded really scared, and I couldn't blame her. After all, none of us wanted to be here or to face Piggy. Piggy was more terrifying than a bear with five shark heads.

"Casey's right!" a big dude said from his spot on the floor. "Man, I've heard about players getting sucked into this game and never coming back. I heard she just yanks players from their servers at random and brings them over to her place here. I never thought that I would actually become one of those victims. I'm Decks, by the way."

"Nice to meet you guys. I'm Noob. I'm a cop at Mad City. I was actually trying to stop a hardware store robbery when I got shot and ended up here. Hang on a minute! I was shot! I was *shot*! Why am I not shot anymore?"

"I hear Piggy has all sorts of crazy powers," someone else said. "Your wound must have healed when you got sucked in here. Unfortunately, Piggy's crazy, and she's going to do a lot worse than shooting you."

Do worse than shooting me? Oh no, I don't know what could be worse than that. Maybe Piggy would hug me to death or insult my ability to play computer games (which is much worse than death).

That was when we saw a huge figure dart out from the corner of the room. The shape was dark, and I couldn't make out who, or what, it was. I instinctively reached for my gun on my hip. My hand fumbled around but found nothing.

"What is that thing?" Casey asked.

"I don't know! But someone's got to do something! You're a cop, Noob! Shoot it!" Danny ordered.

"I would if I had my gun! It's gone!"

"Will you guys get a grip? It's nothing! Just a spider," Decks said.

Decks was right. It was just a spider darting from one cobweb to another. The dim and flickering light made it cast a huge shadow, making it look massive for a moment. In our defense, Piggy could possibly swing from cobwebs too; it seemed like anything was possible with her.

Decks sounded calm and level-headed. With an attitude like that, he would have made a better cop than I did in Mad City.

"No need to scare the cop, Casey. We were all minding our own business until Piggy came and dragged us here. We have to find a way out!" Decks said.

"That's going to be a lot easier said than done, Decks. I've heard that this house may seem small on the outside, but it's a lot larger than it looks. A lot of players have found themselves lost in Piggy's place, never to return again."

"Don't remind us, Danny. We all know that this is a pretty bad situation. We just have to stay positive and try to find a way to get out of here," Casey replied.

Casey was right. It was bad. What we didn't know at that point was that it was about to get a whole lot worse.

"Well, we all agree that we have to get out of this house. The question is, how are we going to do that when we can't get out of this room?" Danny said, pointing out our predicament.

We were locked in. Just as we were discussing the problem, however, we heard a clicking sound, and the door slowly opened. We looked at each other with confusion and suspicion.

"That door was locked! Why is it suddenly open now?" Decks exclaimed.

"Something's definitely not right about the door opening just like that. It's almost as if Piggy wants to get us out of this room," I noted.

"She wants to hunt us down like some kind of sport," Casey agreed.

Danny shrugged his shoulders.

"Probably so, but we really don't have much of a choice. We can't stay in this room forever."

Danny had a point. If we went outside, we would be taking a big risk of running into Piggy, who was almost certainly lurking in the house somewhere. However, staying in the room was not an option either. If only we had some kind of Piggy radar gun.

"I guess we really don't have a choice. We have to try to get out of here," Casey reasoned.

"Yeah. I'd better go out first. I'm the biggest dude around here."

Decks *was* pretty big, but I could tell that he was scared out of his mind at being the first to step out of the room.

Since he was so big, though, he was probably the one who could best handle himself should things get out of hand. I would love to see him wrestle Piggy to the floor like you'd fight over the Xbox controller with one of your younger siblings.

"We're right behind you, Decks," Danny said.

The four of us slowly moved toward the door. Just as he had promised, Decks was the first in line. He slowly pulled on the handle of the door and opened it fully. The door squeaked and creaked and really needed some oiling.

"The coast is clear, guys. There's no sign of creepy Piggy anywhere," Decks confirmed.

"Well, let's get moving then, while we can," Danny responded.

Nothing happened as we filed out of the room. We figured Piggy was biding time before she made her first move. Possibly still sitting in a rocking chair, knitting and plotting like evil grannies normally do.

The room opened onto a long hallway with several other doors. Suddenly, we heard several voices coming from another room.

"Is somebody out there? Help!"

The voices came from behind one of the closed doors.

"There are other players here too!" I said. "We better open that door."

I pulled on the door, but it was locked.

"Please, you have to help me! I don't want to be locked in this room forever!"

"Take it easy! We're going to get you out of there," I shouted back.

"The door's locked. I'm going to have to kick it down."

None of us doubted that Decks could do just that. After all, he was pretty big and strong- looking. Decks could probably fight a herd of elephants with his little finger. He raised his foot and pulled it back. Taking a deep breath, he kicked down the door with one powerful push, sending it flying.

"It's open! Come on!"

Decks rushed into the room, and we followed. There were other Roblox players inside. They all looked pretty relieved to see us and seemed just as frightened as we were.

"Thank goodness! I knew there were other people aside from us in here!"

"How long have you guys been here?" Decks asked.

"I don't know. If you guys are like us, then you would have just been minding your own business, then suddenly you woke up here in this place. We were all locked up in this room together. I'm assuming you guys had a similar experience? I'm Chris, by the way, and these are my friends: Carlos, Pitt, Ricky and Tina."

Chris looked like a very smart guy, and his friends all looked like your average Roblox player. They were all pretty afraid. Yeah, they were just like us. They had all been chilling and playing, doing their own thing, until the mysterious force that was Piggy whisked them away and brought them here. Yeah, we were all pretty unlucky all right.

"Well, I'm Decks, this is Danny SN, that's Casey and this is Noob. It looks like we were all brought together by Piggy somehow."

"I've heard a lot of bad stuff about Piggy," Carlos admitted. "We've all heard about the mysterious force taking Roblox players and sending them to this old house. I never expected to end up a victim myself, though."

"None of us did. We'll all just have to work together to get out of here," I replied.

"Exactly. We'd better stay together and keep moving. Maybe we'll find a way out of this place," Danny offered.

"Sorry, but that doesn't sound like much of a plan," Pitt said snidely.

Danny looked at him with annoyance for a moment before answering.

"All right. Maybe it isn't much, but do you have any better ideas?"

Pitt didn't answer, and neither did his friends. I guess that was their answer. They really didn't have much of a choice; we would all have to stick together if we wanted to have a chance of getting out of this crazy place in one piece. It was like hanging out with your meanest relatives during Christmas.

"Come on. We'd better get moving," Decks insisted.

So, there we were. Several players all stumbling around, trying to find a way out of a maze-like house. It wouldn't be easy to find the exit, but we knew Piggy was sure to strike at any moment.

Entry #2

Exploring Piggy's creepy House.

We wandered around the house for what seemed like forever. Each door seemed to look just like the one before it. The whole wall was like a giant snake that slithered around in a long and endless loop.

"Where are we going? Each door seems to be the same, and the walls seem to go around in circles. This whole dingy house feels like a cramped maze!" Chris exclaimed.

"I know! We've been at this forever! And Piggy hasn't even made her move yet," Tina whined.

"This is getting crazy. We have to do something other than wander around the house like this," Danny agreed.

He was right. If we kept at this, we would never find the way out. We were like little mice going around in circles, and I couldn't shake the feeling that this was exactly how Piggy wanted it to be. DARN YOU, EVIL PIGGY!

"How about we open each door we see?" I sheepishly volunteered. I was really hoping someone else would speak up, but since I already told everyone that I was a cop, I felt I had to prove myself.

"Good thinking, Noob! Let's do that! It's better than wandering around in circles like this," Danny replied.

It was the only logical solution. After all, we couldn't keep going around like this. We had to do something to help us find the way out. I mean, what else was there to do, stay in the room and play charades? I don't think so.

"No way! We don't even know what's behind those doors. One of those rooms is bound to contain a trap... maybe more than one. Who knows what's lurking?" Casey argued.

"No, I agree with Danny and Noob. We're never going to find the way out or discover anything useful if we don't open more doors," Decks said.

No one really liked the idea of opening doors or breaking down locked ones to see what was behind them. The whole house was just plain creepy. Still, no one said anything after Decks spoke. Everyone knew that we didn't really have any choice. It was either explore and risk getting hurt, or just wander around in circles indefinitely.

"You guys are right. We should start opening doors, even if it's scary," Ricky agreed.

"It seems like we're all kind of in agreement then," Tina said.

"Alright, so we open doors. Who's going to stay in front and take the biggest risk?"

"I will. I am the biggest anyway, and I already kicked your door down," Decks said.

No one tried to say otherwise. I was glad that Decks was willing to take the risk. If he wasn't, I really wasn't sure who would go up front.

"Well, we might as well start with this door here," Pitt said, pointing at the door right in front of us. It was closed, like all the other doors in that creepy place. Decks stepped forward with no sign of fear or hesitation. Decks was a big guy; the only problem he had was fitting through the actual door.

"All right, I'm opening it. You guys had better step back or something."

"I'll come with you. It's better that you go in with some help," Chris offered.

Decks nodded and gripped the doorknob. "On three. One, two..."

Decks turned the doorknob. It wasn't locked. The door opened easily, and the two of them stepped into the room.

"All right, turn on the light!" Decks ordered.

I fumbled for the light switch just inside the door and flicked it on. A bright light came over the room that turned out to be the kitchen.

Immediately my eyes caught the stove under an old chimney. The countertop had not been used or cleaned in a while, and it was grimy and covered in dust. There were shelves and cupboards that looked very old. It also smelled quite bad.

It really should have been cleaned a long time ago, but I was sure that Piggy wasn't one for cleaning around the house. By now, we were all sure that Piggy was not one to care much about keeping her house in order. Though it's not like Piggy was unable to clean the house. Supposedly, she had the speed and stamina of an Olympic athlete.

"That's one awfully dirty kitchen! I sure wouldn't want to let my kitchen get like that!" Tina exclaimed.

"I have to confess that my kitchen kind of ended up this dirty once," Casey said.

"Hey, guys, you can compare home-making notes later. Maybe we should all just focus on finding something useful in here," Danny said.

He was right. It was time to get serious and start looking for items that could really be of use against Piggy. After all, from the stories we'd heard about her, she was very dangerous, and we had to be ready for anything.

"I've got a rolling pin. This might come in handy," I said.

It was good for rolling dough, but it would also make a good weapon if need be. Just thinking about it made me squirm a little. I didn't want to use a cooking utensil for such a purpose, but I really didn't have much of a choice. None of us did.

"This might come in handy too," Ricky said.

He grabbed a frying pan. I figured he had the same idea as I did with the rolling pin. If not, then at least he can make an omelet.

"I guess this kettle ought to do," Casey said.

"What's that supposed to do if Piggy attacks?" Danny asked.

"The kettle is full of boiling water. You wouldn't want any of this splashed on your face, right? I figure Piggy won't want any of it on her face either."

"Ouch. Well, you could also make her a nice cup of tea?"

"This oven mitt might be... well, it might be a good boxing glove for fighting Piggy," Pitt said. The last thing Piggy would expect is getting attacked with an oven mitt.

"Were you ever good at any kind of fighting?" Carlos asked.

"Not really, but I'm sure this mitten will be good enough for a pig. I mean, it's sure to hurt if I punch her with it!"

"Yeah, maybe so, but I wouldn't need a glove like that to take her down. If you ask me, I could take on anyone with my bare fists!" Carlos said.

Despite just meeting these people, I could tell that Carlos was the cocky type. He did not bother even trying to look for anything to help him against Piggy. Instead, while we searched, he did some shadow boxing in a corner; it appeared that he really did believe that his fighting skills alone would be up to the task. Maybe he had experience in fighting evil grannies?

"Uhm, no offense, Carlos, but are you sure that you can handle Piggy? I mean, I haven't seen you fight before or anything, and I don't mean to judge, but Piggy's got a pretty fearsome reputation," I said.

"Yeah, I've heard about her reputation. I've heard all sorts of stories about her. I'm sure all of those stories are nothing but crazy tales to scare kids!"

"I don't know about that, Carlos. I mean..."

I was cut short as the lights suddenly went off. We all started shouting. It was worse than any jump scare you could imagine.

"Hey, what's going on?"

"Who turned out the lights?"

"Hey!"

I stumbled around in the dark, just like everyone else, and felt my foot land in something squishy and sticky. I could suddenly smell something horrid.

"Somebody turn on the lights!"

I heard a lot of moving and stumbling, but I couldn't tell what was going on. It was like someone had tossed a giant blanket over us all.

I heard Decks moving around the room. I could tell it was him because it was like hearing a bull moving around in a china shop. I heard the flick of a switch and, finally, the lights came back on.

Everyone squinted and rubbed their eyes as light flooded the entire room again. We looked at each other; something was definitely wrong. I took the opportunity to glance down to see what I had stepped on, and it appeared to be dog poop. There was no dog in the room from what I could see. I think maybe Piggy put it there to mess with us. I didn't want to tell the others out of sheer embarrassment.

"Is everybody okay?" Decks asked.

"I-I think so..." Pitt said, checking himself out as if convinced there was a wound somewhere.

"Wait, where's Carlos?" Casey asked. Everyone stood silent and looked around. There were no signs of Carlos anywhere.

"Carlos! Where are you?" Danny shouted.

There was no reply except the echo of Danny's own voice bouncing. There was an uneasy tension in the room. Everyone knew that something had happened to Carlos... something bad.

"Oh my gosh... Piggy has made her first move... what are we going to do?! Who's going to be next? I knew this was going to end badly for me--"

"Whoa, hold up there! We're not about to leave anyone behind, you got that? We got here as a group and we're going to leave this stinking house as one!" Decks shouted, interrupting Tina's panic.

Decks was definitely the commanding presence in the group, and everyone silently acknowledged him as the leader of our little pack. We all silently nodded our heads in agreement.

"Decks is right. We just need to calm down. I'm sure Carlos is around here somewhere; we've just got to look for him," I said calmly.

Chris had seemed awfully quiet this whole time, and I caught him shaking his head.

"Chris, what's wrong?" I asked him.

"I don't know, dude. I think I've seen this before in a video... Piggy strikes when everyone least expects it. Carlos is a goner, I'm sure of it. And in time... everyone else here will be, too," Chris said grimly.

Chris was probably one of the smarter people in the room, and those words coming from him didn't make any of us feel any better. Maybe I was safe from Piggy since I had dog poop on my shoe and I wouldn't seem like much of a player. Though if she appeared in front of me, I knew that kicking her with my dog poop shoe could be fairly effective.

"Hey, if you're going to be so negative the whole time, then you can stay here in the kitchen and mope all day while you wait for that pig to get you! Otherwise, gather up all the stuff you might need from here and follow me!" Decks commanded.

Before anyone else had time to say anything, we heard the sudden sound of heavy footsteps and creepy laughter in the distance. All our heads turned in the direction of the sound. There was no mistaking it; it was definitely Piggy. I mean, who else could it have been?

Unless some random dude had decided to take a relaxing stroll around this creepy house, it could only mean one thing.... Piggy was nearby.

"W-who was that?!" Tina shouted.

I could tell that she was starting to get really scared by everything that was happening. I mean, we were all scared, no doubt about it. Who wouldn't be, right? But Tina was the worst of us all. It's almost as if I could smell the fear! I bet she didn't like watching scary movies and stuff like that.

"Piggy! Who else could it be? We'd better go check it out!" Decks said.

"Wait! What if that was Carlos?" Pitt replied.

"Impossible! We called for Carlos earlier and he didn't say a thing! That can't have been him!"

"Look, guys, I don't think it matters right now who that was. We'd better get out of this kitchen. The longer we stay here, the slimmer our chances are of breaking out of this creepy place! Let's move!" Danny ordered.

We began to exit the kitchen slowly, each of us following the person in front like a train made up of frightened people. We scanned the corridor and turned in the direction of the sound of footsteps from earlier.

Entry #3

The Secret Door.

We were back in the same hallway again with the doors that all looked the same. Danny and Decks seemed to know where the footsteps had come from, though, so they took the lead, and the rest of us followed them. After passing by several identical wooden doors, we finally stopped at the end of the hallway in front of the last door.

"This is where the footsteps came from, guys," Danny said.

"You sure about that? How can you be absolutely sure that the footsteps came from behind that door?" Pitt asked.

"It's a good guess. It sounded pretty far away when we heard it in the kitchen," Decks explained.

"I don't know, guys... what if Piggy is behind that door? What if she's going to take us all down as soon as we open it?! I'm scared. I don't want to go in!" Tina said, clearly panicking at the thought of what was to come.

None of us wanted to admit it, but we all agreed with Tina. Nobody wanted to face Piggy. There was a long, silent moment. You could have cut the tension in the air with an oven mitt! It was Decks who eventually broke the silence.

"Look, guys, there's no other choice. We've got to go in there. We can't just stay here forever."

Everyone knew that Decks was right, but nobody wanted to admit it. Everyone felt safer in the hallway, but we *couldn't* stay there forever.

Everyone silently nodded their heads and gave Decks the signal to kick the door down. We readied the kitchen utensils that we had grabbed from the kitchen earlier and prepared for the worst. We looked like a bunch of grumpy chefs who wanted to fight a customer who insulted our cooking. Decks took a deep breath one last time and kicked the door down with so much force that it flew across the entire room.

"Freeze!" Decks shouted.

'Freeze'? I'm thinking this dude must have been a cop before he got into this mess with the rest of us! Someone who was so calm and commanding in a crisis had to have had some kind of training. I suddenly felt embarrassed. I was a new cop in Mad City, and I hadn't done anything great so far; I'd just ended up in *this* mess.

We followed Decks into the room and looked around anxiously. There was nothing there. It was completely empty, and there was no proof that Piggy or Carlos had ever even been there. The only thing inside the small room was a really strange-looking, dirty, patterned carpet hung on one of the walls. I thought it could make a great present for my sister.

"There's no one here," Pitt remarked.

"Thank you, Captain Obvious," Chris said with a sarcastic tone.

Pitt glared at Chris but didn't reply. Everyone was busy investigating the small room and looking for clues, hoping to find any sort of sign that could lead us to Carlos, and hopefully the exit. It was too bad. I was really looking forward to seeing him go head to head with Piggy. It would have been hilarious.

"There's nothing here. How could the footsteps have come from this room? They must have come from one of those other rooms we just passed," Casey said.

"Keep looking, guys. There's got to be something in here... like maybe a hidden drawer or door somewhere," Decks insisted.

I stared at the strange, dusty old carpet that hung on the wall and placed my finger on my chin. It was literally the only thing in the room, and I wondered if it was some kind of clue or something. I touched the carpet; it felt really old and ragged, obviously, but I could also feel something else. Something strange. I really hoped there wasn't more dog poop.

"Guys... I think... I think there's something beyond this carpet," I shouted.

The others quickly turned their attention to the carpet in question. Decks closely inspected it like it was some kind of criminal and grabbed one of its ends.

"Only one way to find out," he said.

Decks quickly pulled the carpet with all of his strength, revealing the wall underneath... and a hidden door. It was a really narrow door, so small in fact that I couldn't imagine someone as big as Decks being able to fit through it. I found myself thinking we should have brought some butter from the kitchen so that we could cover him in it and squeeze him through.

"A hidden door!" Pitt exclaimed triumphantly.

"Again, thank you, Captain Obvious," Chris replied.

"What's your problem, man? Why are you always calling me out like that?" Pitt said angrily. I could tell that the tension between these two was increasing at an alarming rate. I anticipated the kitchen utensils being flung around like they belonged to a chef on a tight deadline.

"Ohh... I don't know. Maybe it's because you keep telling us things we already know?"

"Well, Mister Genius Pants, how come I haven't heard you share with us a magical solution that'll get us out of this place?!" Pitt fired back.

"I've got one for you—"

"That's enough!" Decks shouted.

Decks's voice echoed throughout the room, quickly stopping Pitt and Chris in their tracks. Decks was a big dude—

one you didn't want to make angry. He could probably eat you.

"Fighting each other is not going to get us out of this house! We need to work together to get out of this mess! Now, if you two want to throw down and get into a fist fight, then be my guests! But you're both going to be left here if you do, so good luck dealing with that nutcase Piggy on your own!" Decks cried.

"He started it!" Pitt responded childishly.

Decks gave Pitt a glare that could have had a lion shaking in its boots. Pitt got the message and pretty much zipped his mouth from that point on.

The silence was soon broken once again, though, as all of us heard the faint sound of a person crying for help. It was coming from beyond the small door, and we all knew that we had to get in there whether we wanted to or not.

"That sounded like Carlos!" Casey said.

Decks let out a deep sigh and pulled back his leg for another kick. He thrust his foot forward, and the small door immediately caved in. It tumbled down the staircase for what seemed like forever until we finally heard it land deep down in what had to be a basement.

I've got a lot of horrible memories of that crazy staircase. It was narrow and small, just like the door, and the damp and cold gave it a weird smell. The old and awful-smelling walls were made of stone, and it felt like they were about to eat us up and collapse in on each other at the same time.

Everyone in the room gulped and nodded their heads. We all knew that there was a difficult task ahead of us.

"I guess we've got to go down there now," Tina said nervously. I felt like holding her hand, not because she was scared but because I was.

Entry #4

Into the Depths of the Stone Dungeon.

Decks nodded and headed through the door first, although that probably wasn't such a good idea. As the largest one of our group, I noticed that he had a hard time squeezing through the door to the narrow staircase, and an even harder time going down the stairs. We didn't dare say anything about the tight squeeze, though.

One by one, we followed Decks's lead and began to descend the stairs into the cold depths of Piggy's creepy house. The air seemed to get thicker and colder with every step that we took.

After climbing down the stairs for what seemed like an eternity, we finally reached the bottom and saw a large hallway that looked remarkably similar to the one above, although the walls were made of stone like in the staircase. There were some torches on the walls and a number of identical wooden doors all placed next to one another. It was another maze, and it was all part of Piggy's creepy and evil plan.

I swear, if I see another maze in my life, it will be too soon.

"Well, this honestly doesn't look very different from the house upstairs," Chris said.

"Yeah, you want to stay up there? Be my guest, dumb-dumb!" Pitt sneered.

"Why you—"

Before Pitt could say anything further, Chris lunged, and a fist fight broke out between the two of them. Pitt and Chris were both throwing their fists wildly at each other, although I noticed that neither of them was landing any good shots. Clearly, neither was an experienced fighter. They were slapping each other like clowns in a circus or two puppies fighting over a toy.

Before things got any more out
of hand, Decks plunged into the fight
and quickly broke the two apart. Decks
grabbed them both by their shirt collars
and carried them like a sack of potatoes.
Decks was very different to Pitt and
Chris; I could tell that this dude knew
what he was doing. Not only was he big,
but he also knew how to use his size to

his advantage. He probably did some martial arts training camp or something before he got into this mess. I could imagine Decks fighting with a bear on the edge of a mountain. If there was anyone in the group that could stand a chance against Piggy, it was him.

"All right, that's enough! Back it up, you two! I've had just about enough of this nonsense!" Decks said loudly. His voice echoed creepily in the stone hall.

"He keeps messing with me, dude!" Chris fired back.

"He's the one who started it! He said I was dumb and that I kept mentioning the obvious!" Pitt retorted.

"Look, I don't care what your reasons are for fighting—"

"Uhh, guys?"

All of us turned our attention to Danny, who was literally trembling in his shoes. His outstretched finger pointed at something dark in the hallway, and we immediately realized why Danny was so scared.

Standing right there in the distance was Piggy.

She didn't say anything, just stood there like some sort of statue with her glowing red eyes. Pretty much everyone in the hallway was frozen with fear— even Decks. Piggy was going show up sooner or later, and it's not like she was going to tell us before she made her move, but still. It was a shock.

"I-I-It's... G-Piggy!" Tina said. She could barely finish her sentence, and she sounded like she was about to break down with fear.

Decks quickly snapped out of his trance and dropped both Pitt and Chris onto the cold, hard ground. He set off running after Piggy like a cheetah who had just spotted its next meal. Decks could easily eat Piggy like the big bad wolf.

"Come here, you!" Decks shouted as he ran toward his target.

Just as Decks reached Piggy and was about to give her a giant knuckle sandwich, Piggy disappeared into thin air like some kind of mystical ninja.

Decks looked around, confused—there was no trace of Piggy anywhere now.

"H-how did she..? But I thought..."

"It's obviously a trick, Decks. She wants to confuse us into thinking that she's everywhere. She's probably using some kind of magic spell on us. We've got to keep going," Danny explained.

"But how? These doors all look the same, just like upstairs. And there might be traps beyond these doors," Decks replied.

"I have an idea," Ricky said.

Ricky had remained pretty quiet the entire time that we'd been here, so we were all surprised to finally hear him talk.

"Shoot."

"I counted all of the doors while you guys were fighting and all that... and I think I have a plan. There's eight of us here right now, yes? Tina, Decks, Noob, Danny, Casey, Chris, Pitt and me. That's eight people, and there are eight doors," Ricky explained.

"Ohh, I see where you're going with this... so if all of us open one door each, we can cover more distance and hopefully find some kind of exit out of this place. Smart!" Chris told Ricky.

"N-no way! I'm not opening any of those doors! What if Piggy's waiting on the other side of the door that I open?!" Tina said nervously.

"You have to, Tina. It's the only way we can cover ground and get out of here," Pitt replied calmly.

"He's right. And besides, if she does show up when you open your door, just call for help. I'll come crashing in, and I'll beat her up for all that she's done to us!" Decks said angrily.

Decks's last remark seemed to give Tina a little bit of confidence. She took a deep breath and picked a door. The rest of us picked our own, and soon we were all standing in front of our respective doors, waiting to open them at the same time.

"Everyone ready?" Decks called. "Go!"

We pushed open our individual doors slowly. The doors all creaked at the same time, and nobody said a word for a few seconds until Danny finally broke the silence.

"My room is... empty. And it's got another door ahead."

"Mine too," Pitt said. "Same here."

"My room's empty too!" Tina added. Unfortunately, my room wasn't empty. Inside the room was a long and narrow hall. The hall was dimly lit, and I could barely see anything. It probably had a line of dog poop for me to step in. I just knew Piggy wanted to torment me with it.

I hadn't walked far when I felt something clamp down on my leg with a metallic *clank*. It all happened so fast that it wasn't even painful. Well, until it *was*.

I looked down and saw the large bear trap. It had its metal teeth deep in my leg, and there was no way it was letting go. My leg was getting numb now and it was starting to really hurt. And that was when I saw the bear in front of me.

Yeah, everything had led to this terrible moment. I figured that I was going to die right here. I was going to die, not outside in the crazy streets of Mad City, chasing robbers or anything like that. No, I was going to die being eaten alive by a bear, a victim of one of Piggy's most infamous traps. My life flashed before my eyes, and it was mostly of me playing video games. Well, playing video games and eating. I lived a good life.

But fate—and Decks—had other ideas.

The bear was running towards me at full speed, but Decks moved even faster. He came out of nowhere and slammed into the bear, the two of them colliding like runaway trains.

Decks and the bear were locked together in a rolling death grip. Neither of them was about to let go. I felt helpless as I watched the two of them fighting over my life, but what could I do? The bear trap was locked firmly on my leg.

After what seemed like an eternity, the two of them stopped struggling. The bear went limp, and Decks stood up. He looked terrible, but at least he was alive.

"Decks! You did it!" I cried.

"Yeah, and I don't want to do anything like that again."

"No argument here, but how did you defeat that bear?"

"Just a lucky coincidence, I guess. I've been carrying around a tranquilizer dart ever since I visited Pet Simulator back in the day. I had a hunch it would in handy sooner or later. Apparently, I was right."

"No argument here again. But I guess I'm done for, anyway."

"What do you mean?"

I pointed at my bloody leg and the bear trap.

"I'm snared. Unless you've got a sledgehammer or something like it, I'm not going anywhere."

Decks shook his head.

"There's no way I'm leaving anyone behind. I may not have a sledgehammer, but I might have something just as good."

He whipped out a rusty key. "Where did you get *that*?" I asked. The dude was full of surprises.

Remember when I saw Piggy earlier and I tried to punch her and I missed and she disappeared? Well, Danny said that it was all a trick, but it wasn't. Not in the way we thought. She was no illusion. That was the real Piggy. I managed to get close enough to her to pick her pocket."

I couldn't believe what I was hearing! Decks must have had experience doing bank heists or something.

"You used to be a pickpocket or something?"

Decks smiled at me.

"Guilty as charged. You learn a lot of things growing up on the mean streets of Mad City."

"You sure you should be telling all of this to a Mad City cop?"

Decks shook his head.

"No, but I'm not going to let anyone die in a place like this. I was a petty thief back in the day, not a killer. Now, let's just hope this key is the right fit for that bear trap. It could be the key to anything."

Decks bent down and used the rusty key on the trap. I heard it squeak as it turned. Decks fiddled with the key a little longer, and then I was free! I howled in pain.

At the sound, everyone came rushing through the door.

"Whoa! That looks really bad!" Danny said.

"Move over. I used to be a doctor before all of this craziness," said Tina. She bent to examine my wound.

"It's not that bad. Decks, take off your shirt. I'll need you to tear it up. I can tie up the wound with it and minimize the bleeding."

Decks followed orders. Tina wrapped the cloth around my bleeding leg, fashioning a crude bandage.

"There, that should stop the bleeding. You're lucky, Noob. Although that bear trap looked menacing, it wasn't meant to kill. The real killer would have been that bear in front of you. Some antibiotics and a hospital, and you'll be fine—assuming you get out of here alive, of course."

"Of course. And Tina, Decks, thanks. I owe you both."

Decks shook his head.

"Forget it. Now, let's get moving. I want to get out of here."

We went back to investigating each door. Pretty soon, everyone realized that the room behind their door simply led to another room... and another... and another... and another. A true labyrinth.

This Piggy person was crazy indeed! She wanted to drive us crazier than a farmer trying to play chess with a free-range chicken.

"How are we going to get out now? This is endless!" Pitt cried.

Before anyone could reply, the sound of Decks's loud voice crackling inside the maze filled the air.

Entry #5

Two Down, Seven More to Go...

"Guys! Guys! Come here! Carlos! He's here!"

Everyone quickly retraced their steps and made their way to Decks. It wasn't easy—the maze was really confusing, and every room looked the same—but the sound of Decks's voice eventually led us to our destination.

"Carlos! Carlos! Wake up, man!" Decks shouted.

Stepping inside the room, we quickly noticed one thing that made this room stand out from the rest: a boiling pit of lava that separated us from Carlos! The pit was the entire width of the room, and the only way to get across was to jump over it. Except it looked *way* too far to jump. I suddenly felt a wave of nervousness overcome me; I wasn't good at jumping! One mistake and I'd fall to my death!

We all kept calling Carlos's name, but he didn't respond. I noticed a big red lump on his head; clearly Piggy had whacked him pretty hard with something.

Carlos eventually regained consciousness and awoke slowly, looking dazed.

"H-huh... Where am I..? Arghh! My head hurts!" Carlos said as he sat up and began rubbing his temples.

"Carlos! Thank goodness you're awake! Can you hear me?" Decks shouted.

"Yeah, man... I can hear you loud and clear. What's going on?"

"You're in Piggy's house, remember? I'm Decks, and you were trapped with everyone else in the group. Then the lights went out and Piggy kidnapped you," Decks reminded him.

"Y-yeah... I think I can remember now... I don't remember how I got here, though. And what's that boiling pit of lava doing there?" Carlos said. I wanted to make a sarcastic joke about the lava actually being soup to help lighten the mood... but I managed to hold back.

"I don't know. We're at the very bottom of Piggy's house right now. Do you think you can jump across here? We'll try to find an exit together," Decks said.

"Oh yeah, for sure. Pffft. Look at that lava pit. This will be easy. You guys do know that I'm a star basketball player, right?" Carlos said arrogantly. Clearly, the knock to his head hadn't gotten rid of his overinflated ego. What, was he going to dribble his way out of the situation?

We all looked at each other and shook our heads.

"Aww, come on! Don't tell me you guys don't play Basketblox! I'm the biggest star there! Did you hear about the time when I—"

"Would you just shut up and jump already?!" Danny cried.

Carlos shrugged and stood up. He squatted down low, preparing himself for the big jump across the lava pit. All of us were cautiously hopeful that he'd make it across after his boasting. But Carlos made one very big mistake.

He forgot to tie his shoelaces!

Rather than jumping across the pool, Carlos instead slipped forward into the boiling lava. It all happened so quickly. Everyone shouted and stared in horror as Carlos was disappeared from view.

"Carlos! Nooooo!" Decks shouted desperately.

Decks reached out his hand in order to pull Carlos from the pit, but it was too late. In just seconds, Carlos's body had disappeared faster than toilet paper down the... well, toilet.

"Oh my gosh! Nooo! This is getting crazy! I've got to get out of here!" Tina screamed as sweat trickled down her forehead. She was freaking out so much that it was scaring the rest of us. I took the opportunity to let out a little fart during the commotion. I had been holding it in since we entered the room.

Tina turned back toward the door and started to make a run for it. She hadn't noticed the pebble in front of her.

In her panic, she slipped on the stone and quickly slid backward into the lava pit.

"Arghhh! Help me!" Tina screamed desperately.

First Carlos and now Tina?!

OK, I know games can get pretty violent these days. But this? This was way beyond the scope of what I was prepared to see.

This was really getting out of hand. Piggy was probably laughing somewhere in the dark. This was not good. Not good at all. Piggy knew that lava pits were a Roblox player's biggest nightmare, after spiders with wings or penguins with rocket launchers. Or is that just me?

"That's two down... seven more to go," Ricky said grimly.

"Why are you being so negative about this, man?! We'll get out of this alive, you'll see!" Chris said.

I could tell that Chris was also really scared but was doing his best to stay strong for the rest of the group. I had to admit, though, Ricky was right.

We were two people down, and Piggy probably didn't intend to let any of us out of her madhouse. The big question was: who was going to be next? I gulped at the thought of being burned by Piggy. I had to stay alive somehow... I had to get out of this place in one piece!

"Look, guys, everyone calm down! Look what happened to Tina when she started to panic! There's a way out of this place, but we just have to stay calm!" Decks shouted.

"Calm?! Are you serious, man? We just saw two people get burned alive because of Piggy's traps! Who's to say we're not next?!" Pitt shouted desperately.

"You want to go jump in the lava pit? Then be my guest! But our best chance of surviving is by staying calm!" Decks fired back.

"Decks is right. Let's exit this room calmly and slowly. There must be another room that leads to some sort of exit somewhere," Danny insisted.

But there wasn't.

Once we were out of the boiling lava pit room, we thoroughly searched the other rooms in the hopes that we would find a door that would lead us out of Piggy's house. But there was no such door. All the rooms simply led on to other rooms, and finally, after what felt like hours of searching and opening doors, everyone gave up and realized that there was only one way out of the dungeon unless we wanted to go back upstairs, back to square one. We had to go through the lava pit.

"We've been searching these rooms for hours! They just lead to more rooms and even more rooms! This is crazy! We're going to starve to death down here if we don't do something soon!" Pitt said.

"For once, I've got to agree with you," Chris said. "We can't keep doing this forever. These rooms are just leading us nowhere. The only logical place to go now is across the lava pit. It's the only place we haven't explored yet."

Decks, strangely enough, was the only person who didn't seem to like the idea, even though he was the bravest of all of us.

"No, no, no! We're not going back there! There has to be a way out of this place in one of these rooms! Probably some kind of secret entrance just like how the carpet was hiding the door," Decks insisted.

"Look, Decks, we can't do this forever. We've been at this for hours now. There's clearly no trap door or secret entrance anywhere in these rooms; just concrete and even more concrete! We have to jump over the lava pit! It's the only way!" I said.

Decks scowled and shook his head. He started to sway from side to side as though he was starting a dance routine.

"Hey," I said. "I dance when I'm scared too! But I think Chris is right, Decks. We've already lost Carlos and Tina. We'll all lose each other here if we don't make our move!"

Decks stopped dancing and reluctantly nodded his head. He obviously didn't like the idea, but he was outnumbered. None of us wanted to jump over the lava pit, but there was no other choice — it was either that or wait and starve to death. I'd sooner take my chances with the lava pit.

Danny was the first one to make the jump. To be honest, I didn't think Danny would be able to make it, but he sure proved me wrong. I didn't think that someone who spent his spare time on YouTube would have the athletic skill to jump across a boiling pit of lava, but who was I to say? He did it, and he did it pretty well! He was like an elegant horse that escaped a farm for the first time.

Decks went next. Jumping to the other side was nothing for Decks. His huge, muscular legs easily propelled him into the air, and he landed with a loud thud on the concrete on the other side of the boiling lava pit. Decks had legs like the Incredible Hulk; it was no surprise that he was able to make the jump.

One by one, with encouragement from Decks and Danny, the others in the group also successfully made the jump. I was the last to attempt it, and I was *super* scared. I mean, who wouldn't be? One wrong move and I would easily end up like Carlos or Tina.

"Come on, Noob, you can do it!" Casey called out.

"Yeah, don't worry about it. Everyone else made it. We've got your back," Decks shouted.

I looked down at the boiling pit of lava one last time and took a deep breath.

"Here goes nothing," I said.

I squatted down and pushed off from the ground as hard as I could. It was a pretty good attempt, and I would have easily made it past the pit. There was one problem, though...

I slipped.

I was just as clumsy as Tina and Carlos. Once again, the world felt like it was moving in slow motion, and I found myself falling fast toward the pit of lava. I knew that it was the end, so I simply closed my eyes and prepared for the worst.

Entry #6

Don't Slip, Don't Fall!

Just when I thought that I was about to get burned alive, I felt someone's hands grip my shoulders. It was Decks. His grip on me was really, really tight as he attempted to save me from my fiery fate. Think of an eight-foot crab that just grabbed you with its giant iron pincers or something.

"Oh no you don't! I've already lost two people; I'm not about to lose another one!" Decks cried.

With his great strength, Decks lifted me up as if I were as light as a feather and tossed me into the concrete wall. It wasn't the optimal landing, but hey, it was a lot better than getting burned alive.

"Ouch!"

"Sorry about that, Noob. I had to make sure you were as far away from the lava pit as possible."

"Great! We've all made it. We'd better keep going... We just might make it out of this alive!" Danny said happily.

We looked around for an exit and noticed a small door behind us. It creaked as the others had earlier as we opened it cautiously. But this one wasn't like the others, where the rooms simply led to other rooms... No, this one was very different.

It was a cavernous room... You might call it a *pit*. Where the floor should have been, there was only a gigantic hole, so deep that it appeared endless. The only way we could get across was to walk over a narrow wooden beam. There were no rails to hold on to; we simply had to balance ourselves and hope that we wouldn't fall into the deep dark below.

We all froze at the sight of the small walkway. It was so narrow that you had to place one foot on the beam at a time or else you'd fall below.

"What is this?!" Chris cried out.

"It looks like some kind of really, really narrow bridge... I think I can see a door at the end of it, though," Pitt observed.

"This is insane! That walkway is way too narrow. We'll never get across!" Casey said, panicking.

"Not if we do it really, really, really slowly," Decks said reassuringly.

Decks was going to have the hardest time getting across the bridge since he was the biggest. He would have to balance his weight on the walkway, and that wouldn't be easy.

After a few minutes of silence, Decks broke the tension.

"Look, we've gotten this far, right? I mean, we found the secret dungeon, we found Carlos, we made it across the lava pit, and now we're here. There's no turning back. We have to move," Decks said grimly.

"This is all part of Piggy's evil plan... We've got to make her pay somehow, guys!" I said.

"Don't worry, dude. I'm sure we'll get out of this place, one way or another," Danny told me with a pat on the shoulder.

He smiled at me, and that was all the encouragement I needed to get across. I mean, hey, if a big YouTube star believed in me and in the rest of us, then why shouldn't we believe in ourselves?

Decks took his first steps on the narrow walkway, and the rest of us quickly followed him. Each of us cautiously took one step at a time, making our way across very slowly. One wrong step and we could all fall to our doom, and that knowledge hung over us like a guillotine.

Our strategy seemed to be working; I was surprised to see that we were all making pretty good progress. In fact, I could clearly see the door on the other side, and we were already halfway across. Everything was going great...

Until Decks slipped.

His foot was just too big. It caught the edge of the narrow walkway, and the rest happened so fast.

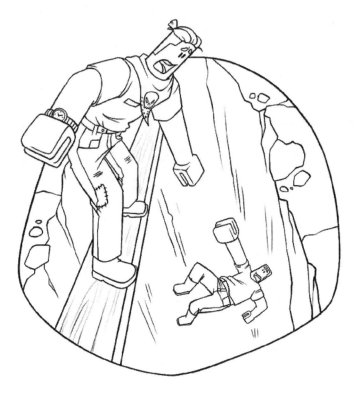

As Decks fell, I saw Pitt, Chris, and Casey grab him to try to pull him back up onto the walkway... but Decks was just too heavy. Ricky, Danny, and I watched in horror as four of our new friends fell to their doom. We heard their cries as they fell deeper and deeper into the endless cavern of darkness.

"Noooooo!"

"Heeeeeeelp!"

"Ahhhhh!"

I tried to reach out for their hands, but it was too late. Danny instinctively pulled me back and gripped my shoulders.

"No! Don't even try, dude! It's too late for them! We've got to keep going. We're almost across, man," he said.

"But those guys were our friends!" I protested.

"So were Carlos and Tina. It's just the three of us now. And the only way to help them now is by making that evil, crazy porker pay," Ricky said angrily.

He was right. There was no way we could save our friends now. It was much too late for them. Piggy had to pay for all of this, one way or another. I was ready to dropkick her in the face.

After a few more tense moments, Ricky, Danny, and I successfully crossed the narrow walkway and made it over to the wooden door. All three of us breathed a sigh of relief, and boy was I thankful that I was one of the lucky ones who had made it this far.

Entry #7

The Final Fight.

"This is it, guys. This is the moment when we put an end to all of this," I said to Ricky and Danny.

"Wait, what? How can you be sure that this is the last room? We walked through countless rooms," Danny said.

"Well, uh... I don't know, really. I've just got this gut feeling that this is it. Yeah, maybe I'm wrong, but whatever. It's worth a shot," I told them both.

Ricky and Danny took out the kitchen implements they had chosen earlier and readied themselves for a fight. Ricky took out the frying pan, and Danny took out a large wooden spoon.

I took out my own weapon of choice... the rolling pin. A frying pan, a wooden spoon, and a rolling pin. Not exactly weapons of mass destruction, but better than trying to fight with just our bare hands. A little better, at least.

Through the door was a stone room, just like all the others, although this time it was much bigger. Much, much, much bigger. There were no precarious walkways, boiling lava pits, or extra doors inside. Nope, it was just a huge stone room with four torches attached to the walls on each side of us. And who was in the middle of it? You guessed it. The villain of the night: Piggy herself.

"Well now, boys... I'm surprised you made it this far. I didn't think that anyone would actually get past all my traps and make it here," she said menacingly. There was something weird about the way in which she spoke; her high-pitched voice made her sound a lot like a bird talking.

"You're going to pay for all the people you've taken down, Piggy!" Danny shouted.

"We'll see about that. See, now that you're here, you can freely exit the house through a final door that's hidden within this room... but it will only show itself if you can beat me!" Piggy said, letting out an evil laugh.

Danny and Ricky had heard enough. They'd suffered enough, and they'd had enough. They weren't about to talk to this crazy pig any longer. Both of them charged toward her with their kitchen utensils in their hands, ready to fight.

And then the most incredible thing happened. Right before our eyes, Piggy multiplied. I mean literally! Suddenly, there were three Grannies to take care of, and each looked more evil than the last.

I saw the shock on Danny and Ricky's faces, but I had to admit, they reacted fast. They separated and went for the two Grannies on the sides, leaving me to fight the one in the middle.

I took a deep breath and ran ahead, hoping to end things with one swift blow. But Piggy was a lot faster than I had expected. She moved like a ghost and immediately knocked me down. I hadn't even done any damage yet, and I was literally shaking in my boots. I could feel that the end was near, much like that time I forgot to bring my homework to school.

"W-wait, p-please! Have mercy! I used to have a totally awesome life in Roblox! I should never have become a cop! Never! I just can't do this kind of stuff! I'm too young to get whacked in the head with a baseball bat by some creepy farm animal!" I pleaded.

Yeah, I know how that came out. I looked and sounded like a total wuss. A coward. A yellowbelly. The list of awful names could go on and on. But I was terrified, and I just couldn't help myself. Being in that situation was just too horrifying; no amount of training could have prepared me to face the monster that was Piggy.

But Piggy didn't care. She didn't care if I, or any of her victims, were scared stiff. In fact, she enjoyed all of this. If she was once human, she certainly was not anymore; she was something else entirely now. And I would have to face this monster with nothing but my rolling pin.

She dived straight at me like an eagle that had spotted its target. Without thinking, I quickly reached for the rolling pin that I had taken earlier and used it as a shield against Piggy's attacks. I know what you're thinking: what good could a rolling pin do against a baseball bat? I know, it was a silly idea... but it actually worked. Piggy was about to nail me, but she stopped dead in her tracks when she caught a glimpse of the rolling pin.

"Nooo! What are you doing with my rolling pin?! That's the same rolling pin I've used to make cookies for Slendrina! Give it back!" Piggy ordered.

Piggy grabbed the end of the rolling pin and began to pull. I pulled back, and a small tug of war ensued between the two of us. While we were both fighting for the rolling pin, the other two Grannies suddenly evaporated. It was clear that mine was the real Piggy now, so Danny and Ricky had to come help me.

Thankfully, I watched them both hurl themselves straight at Piggy. She never saw it coming. Ricky began whacking her with the frying pan, and Danny used his wooden spoon.

It was a really strange sight, seeing two guys beating up a crazy animal with kitchen utensils, but I can't say she didn't deserve it... not after what she had done to our friends earlier. And it didn't seem like the guys were doing much damage anyway.

Piggy was still fighting me for the rolling pin when suddenly her hat fell off. At first, I thought that meant we'd hit her with a devastating blow, but then I realized that it was the *shoes* you're supposed to check. And Piggy's shoes were still on.

Still, there was no escape for Piggy now, and she knew it. Unable to let go of the rolling pin, at some point Piggy fell to the floor and collapsed. She had taken a pounding from Danny and Ricky, and she was done.

"W-what happened?! Is it over?" Danny said as he looked around, partially concussed and confused about what had happened.

"I think we beat her," Ricky said.

"Yeah, guys! You totally did it! You beat that jerk!" I said.

I was so relieved. I'd absolutely had it with this terrible place and the many death traps inside. The dark corners, the rotting floors, overgrown spiders, *lava pits*... All that was done. We were all going to survive our encounter with Piggy!

Or were we?

It was a little early for us to celebrate, but we all realized this too late. It turned out that Piggy wasn't done with us. Not by a long shot.

Ricky didn't even see it coming. None of us did. That demented pig moved so fast, it seemed unnatural for, well, a demented pig. Somehow, she kicked Ricky from behind. I knew that Ricky was not getting up from the hit. Another one of us down, and in the most unexpected manner.

"Ricky, no!"

Ricky wasn't answering, and he wasn't moving. Piggy had taken another victim.

I raised my rolling pin to smash her the way she had smashed Ricky, but it was no use. Piggy moved fast and swung hard. Her baseball bat struck my rolling pin and snapped it in two. All Danny and I could do was stare. Piggy had unbelievable strength.

Then again, she had a lot of unbelievable stuff going for her. So it wasn't *that* hard to believe.

Like I said before, she was like some kind of inhuman creature. I mean, this was way beyond the scope of your regular Piggy being cranky because she missed a nap.

I rushed again at Piggy, but she was too fast. She struck me in the gut with her baseball bat, and I instantly felt the wind knocked out of me. I couldn't breathe, and I doubled up in pain, collapsing on the ground and clutching my stomach.

"You crazy old monster! You're going to pay for all of this! You're going to pay!"

Danny was enraged now. He rushed at Piggy, which turned out not to be the smartest thing to do. In fact, it was just about the worst thing he could have done.

Why? Because Piggy was standing in front of the wall, and right before Danny was about to tackle her, she used her unnatural speed to move out of the way. Danny hit the wall with a *thud* that made me wince.

Ouch.

In the meantime, I was still lying on the floor, in too much pain to even try to stop Piggy.

After what seemed like an eternity, Piggy turned toward me.

"Both your friends are done for, fool. Now, it is your turn."

Seeing my sorry state, she took her sweet time ambling over to me. What was she about to do with me?

One thing was certain—she wasn't about to make me an apple pie and let me go.

"You're all going to pay. All of you," Piggy said.

Her voice sounded like something between broken glass and a crow cawing.

"Why are you doing this? What did we ever do to you?"

Piggy shook her head. She was in no mood to give me answers.

Once again, I pretty much thought that I was done for. But that was when the unexpected happened.

"Hey, ugly! I'm not through with you yet!"

I heard the familiar voice from behind Piggy.

It couldn't be! How was this possible? Piggy turned around, her face a picture of shock. Behind her stood Decks.

"You? You fell into the bottomless pit! How are you even still alive?"

I had *seen* Decks fall into that bottomless pit with our other friends with my own eyes. Decks should have been done for, but he wasn't. Somehow, he had managed to climb out, and he now stood in front of Piggy, face to face.

I could see that there was something different about Decks. He looked a lot more haggard and beaten up than last time I'd seen him, just a few minutes earlier, as if he had gone through a meat grinder. But there was something more. There was something different about the way Decks stared at Piggy.

It seemed like Decks was no longer afraid.

He stared down the beast like his eyes could burn holes through her. Decks wasn't backing down; he was now fearless.

"No one's ever survived the bottomless pit. No one!" Piggy shrieked.

Decks grinned and laughed softly at Piggy. It seemed as if he were laughing at death itself. Hearing Decks, I actually felt more afraid of him at that moment than of Piggy.

"Yeah, well, I guess I'm no one then."

Decks whipped out a deck of cards. How big were this dude's pockets? At the sight of them, Piggy seemed genuinely terrified.

"The cards of fate! How did you get a hold of them?"

Decks shook his head. "I don't need to answer any of your questions."

Decks pulled out a card from the deck and tossed it at Piggy. He tossed the card so fast, I barely managed to follow it with my eyes. The card struck Piggy's hand. It cut her, and she drew back in great pain. She dropped her baseball bat to clutch her wounded hand.

"Yaaah! You cut me!"

"I'm going to do a lot more than just cut you, Piggy. You're done for!"

Decks whipped out another card and tossed it Piggy's way. The second card was more powerful than the first.

It struck Piggy right in the chest, and something unbelievable happened.

Piggy exploded. It was as if Decks had tossed a bomb her way.

It was a small, controlled explosion that had just enough power to take Piggy out. The entire house remained untouched, and I was also unharmed. When the smoke cleared, there was nothing left of Piggy. She had just evaporated.

"Whoa! Decks! You're... you're alive," I said.

Decks shrugged. He still had the cards of fate held firmly in one hand.

"Yeah, I am."

"That's incredible! You're alive and you defeated Piggy! That's... I just can't believe it!"

I had really thought that I would never see Decks again.

"Hey, maybe I'm just a lot tougher to kill than I look."

Decks was being coy, but I had to know how he'd managed to survive such a fall.

"How did you do it, Decks? And what are those cards?"

Decks was reluctant to provide answers. He just shook his head and stared at me. There was no hate in his eyes, but his gaze was as firm as it was with Piggy earlier. So I decided to just leave it at that.

After all, it was hard to argue with a man who had just done was I'd seen Decks do. He had the cards stacked in his favor, literally.

"All right, I guess I don't need to know," I conceded.

"Piggy's done. We should be able to get out of here now."

We both suddenly caught a glimpse of a door that seemed to have magically appeared out of nowhere. This door was different from the others. Through its transparent windows we could see the most awesome thing ever. I immediately recognized the buildings and structures outside; this was the skyline of Mad City.

I don't know how it happened, but somehow the house was just outside of Mad City now. I'll never fully understand that house, or Piggy; it was as if both were magical things born out of pure evil. We had found freedom at last, and it was waiting for us just beyond the door. We had done it! We beat Piggy and put her in her place!

"It's over. It's really over then. We can finally walk out of here," I said.

"Yeah, I guess it is. We were the only ones to make it out alive."

We stepped outside and saw Mad City up ahead. It would be a bit of a walk to get there, but Decks and I didn't mind. We were just relieved to be alive.

"Is she really gone for good? Piggy I mean," I asked.

Decks gave me his signature shrug.

"Piggy and that house were like evil spirits or a virus or something. They can appear anywhere, and you can't really kill something like that," he said.

We turned around and saw that the house had vanished. Decks's words were already making sense.

"What are you going to do now?" I asked Decks.

Decks smiled at me and nodded at the pack of cards he still carried in his hand.

"I think I'll put these things to good use. After all, I did almost die back there to get them. A cop and a petty thief, the only survivors of Piggy's house of horrors. Kind of ironic, isn't it?"

I couldn't argue with Decks. Strange, but it had to just be a coincidence, right? I mean, it wasn't like I would ever see Decks again.

"You're not going to go after me after all of this, are you?" Decks asked.

I smiled and shook my head.

"No way. You saved my life back there. Besides, I've probably got a lot more pressing things to do now."

Decks held up the cards of fate with pride. "Pressing stuff? Like what?"

"I'm going to try and find my partner, and eat as many donuts as Robloxly possible."

And that's how the crazy adventure with Piggy ended.

Sure, we may have lost a lot of friends in the process, but hey, they probably just respawned somewhere else and are living their best lives right now. I hope so, at least.

The important thing was that we did something that so many other players had failed to do: we defeated Piggy, escaped her house, and lived to tell the tale.

Follow Noob's adventures in Diary of a Roblox Noob: Bee Swarm Simulator.

Robloxia Kid

If you enjoyed this book, please leave a review on Amazon! It would really help me with the series.

Best, Robloxia Kid

Made in the USA
Columbia, SC
03 December 2024

48344882R00083